I Want a Pet!

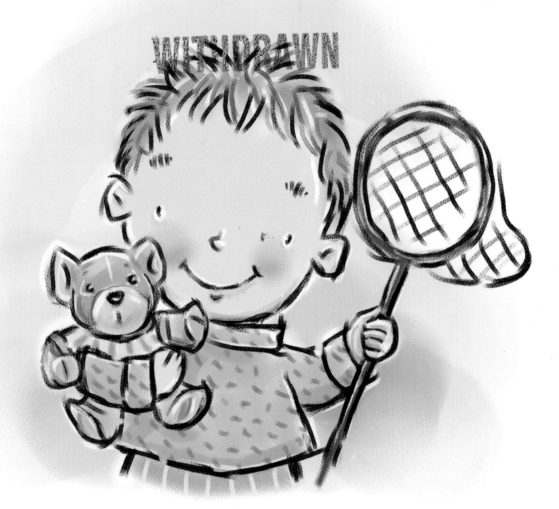

by Cathy Morrison

tiger tales

I want a pet.

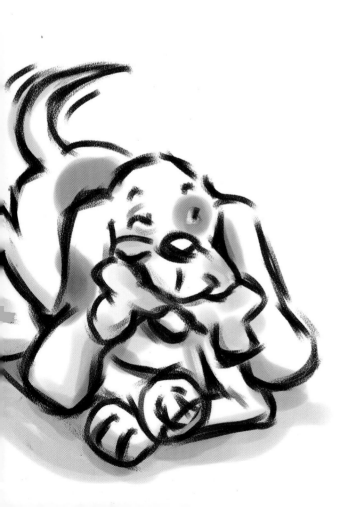

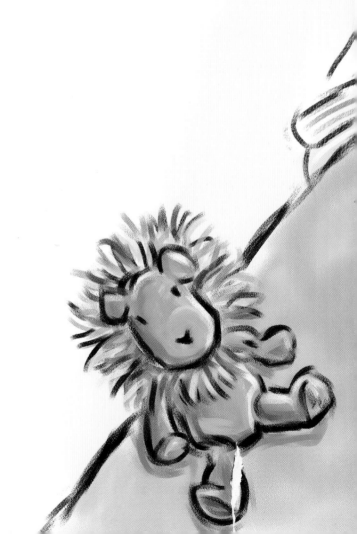

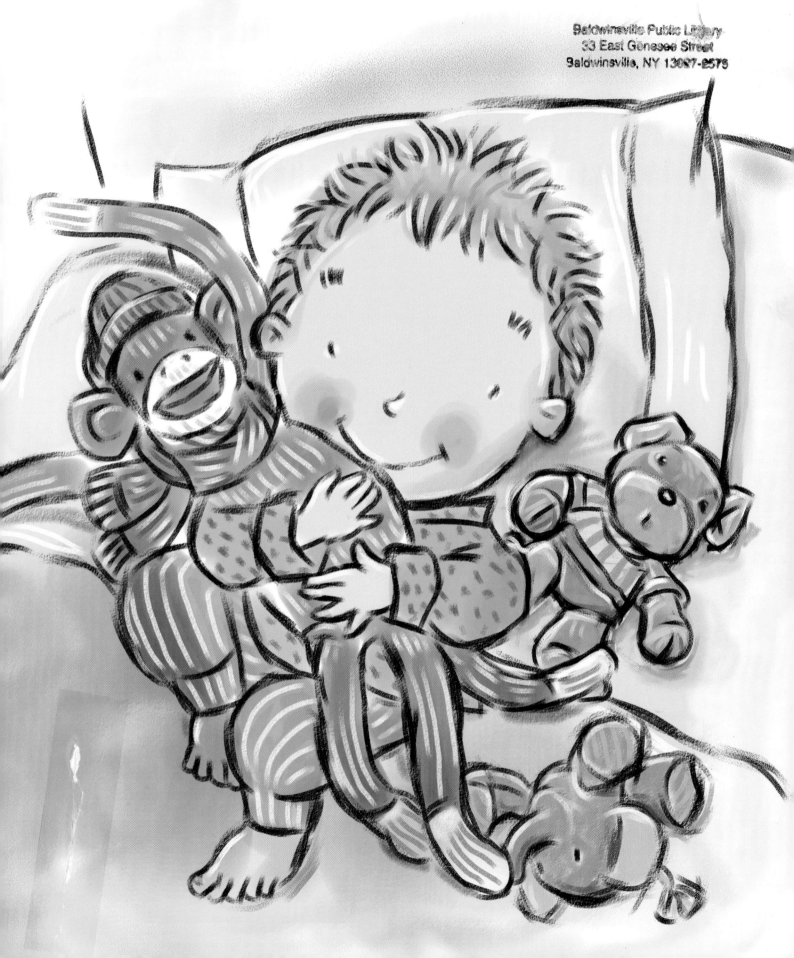

Not just any
pet will do.

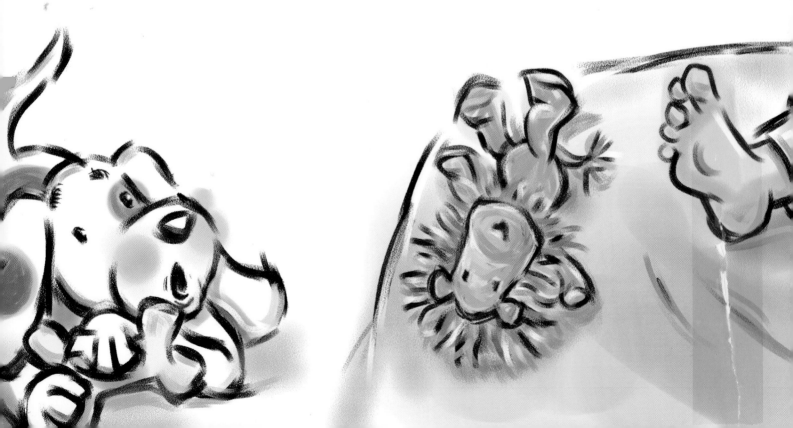

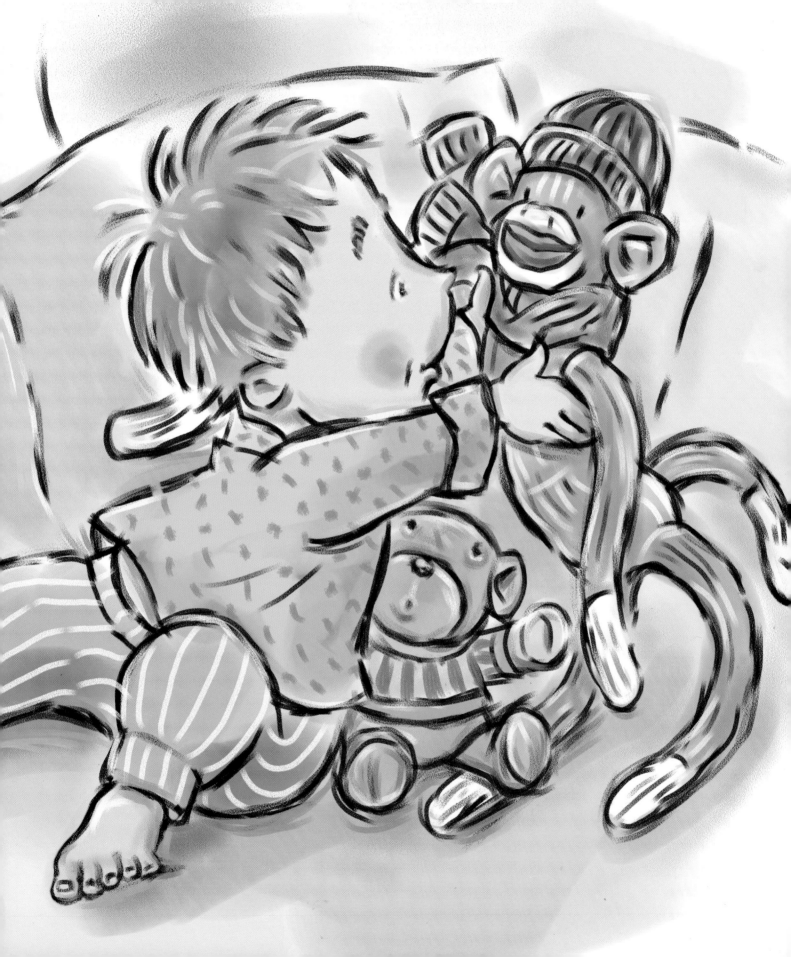

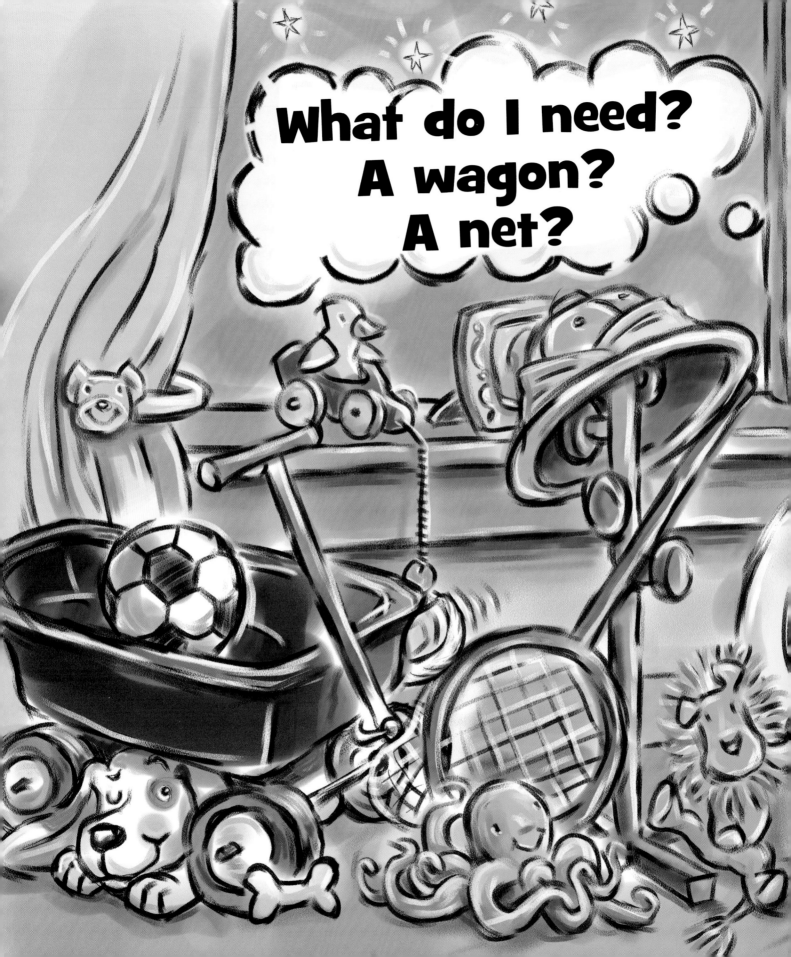

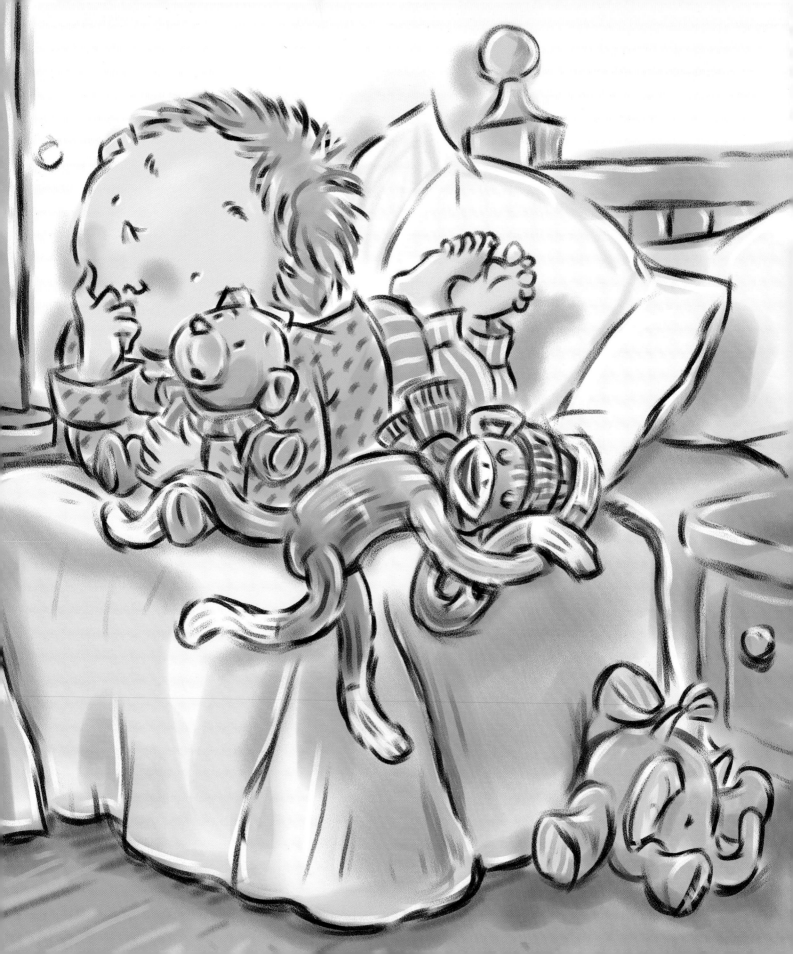

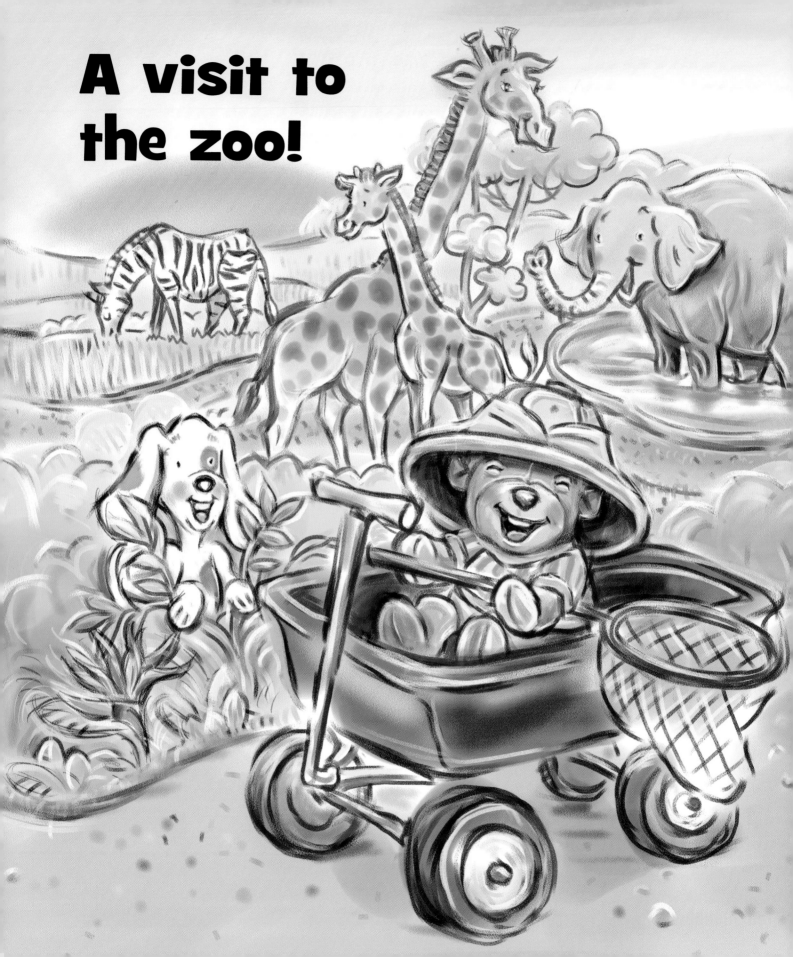

A visit to
the zoo!

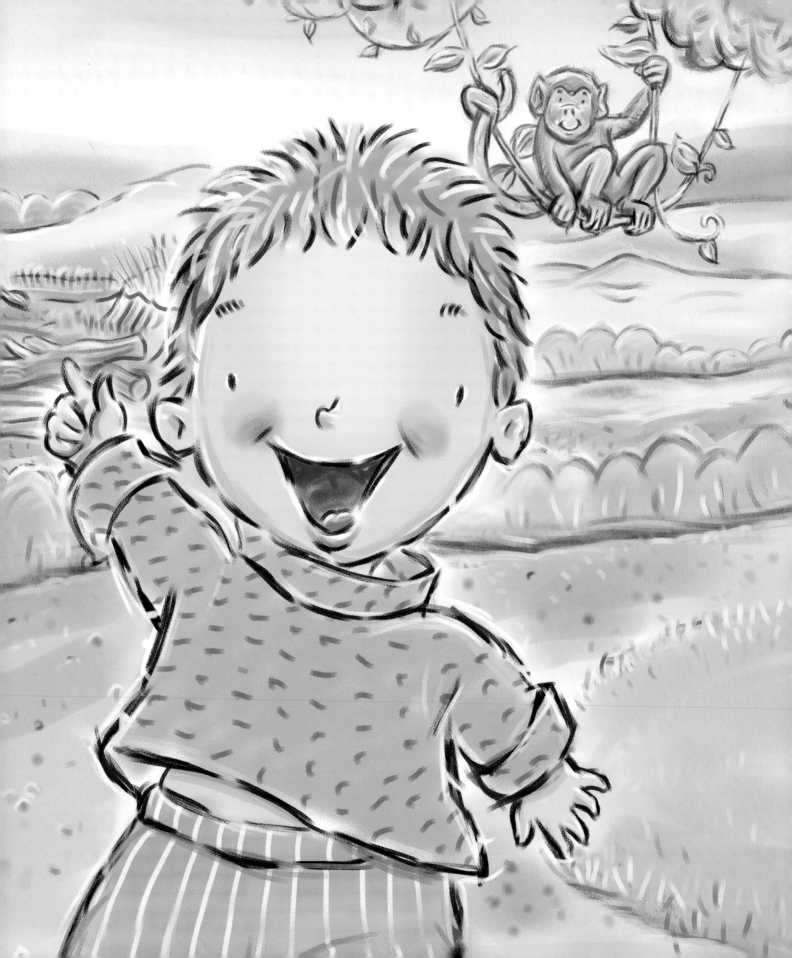

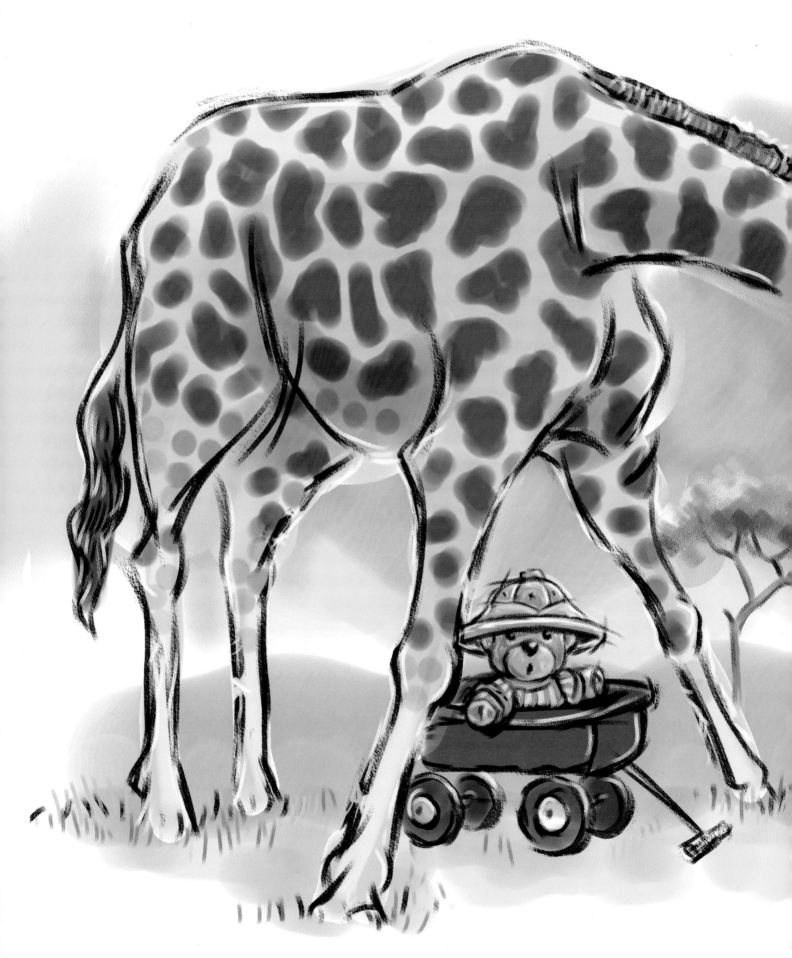

Too high.

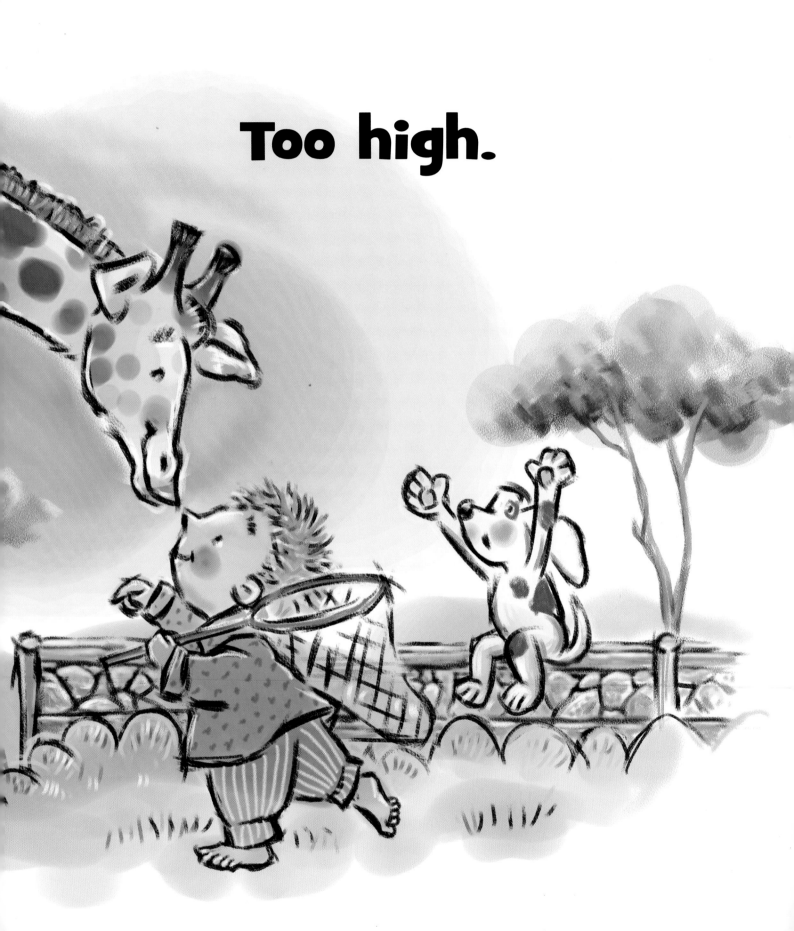

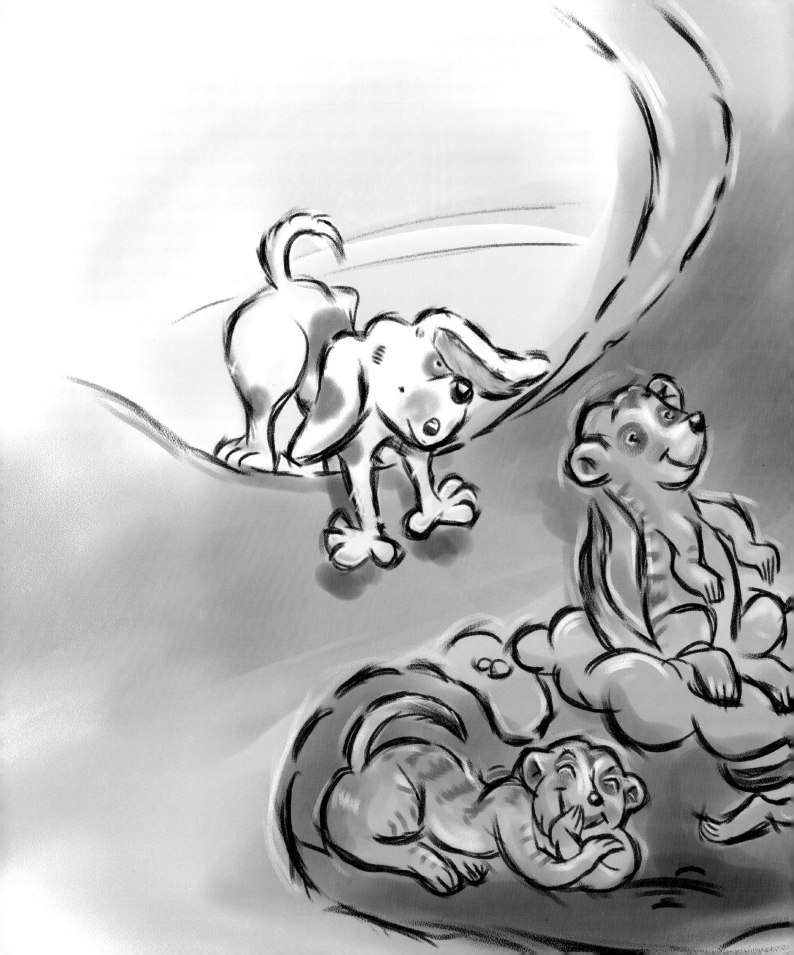

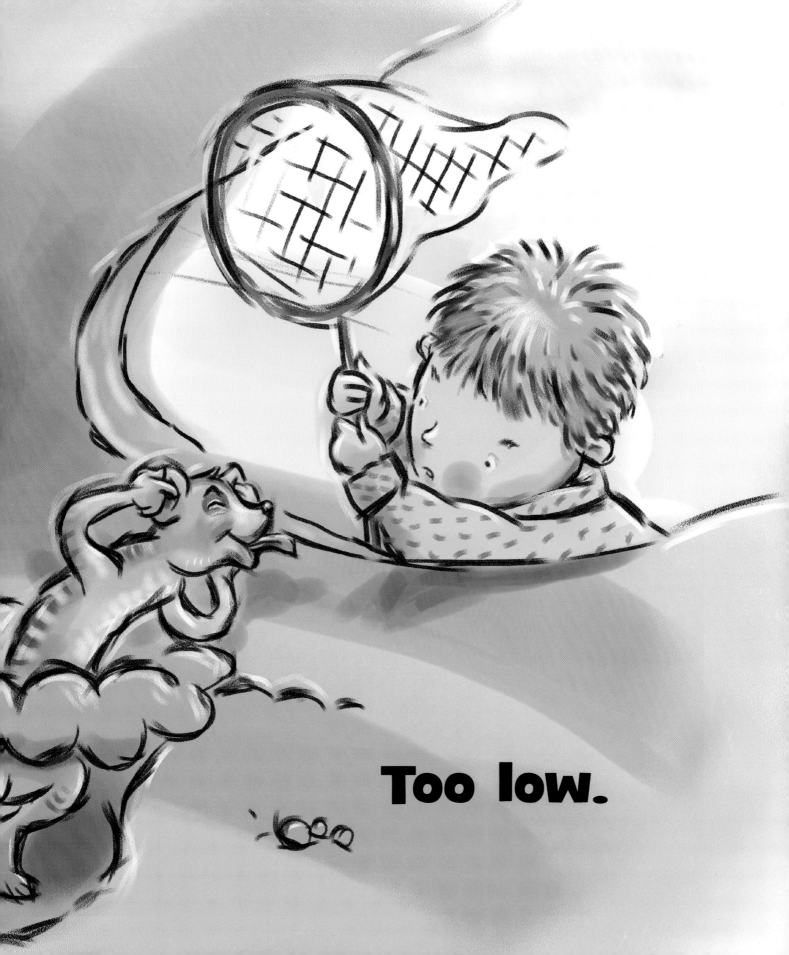

Too low.

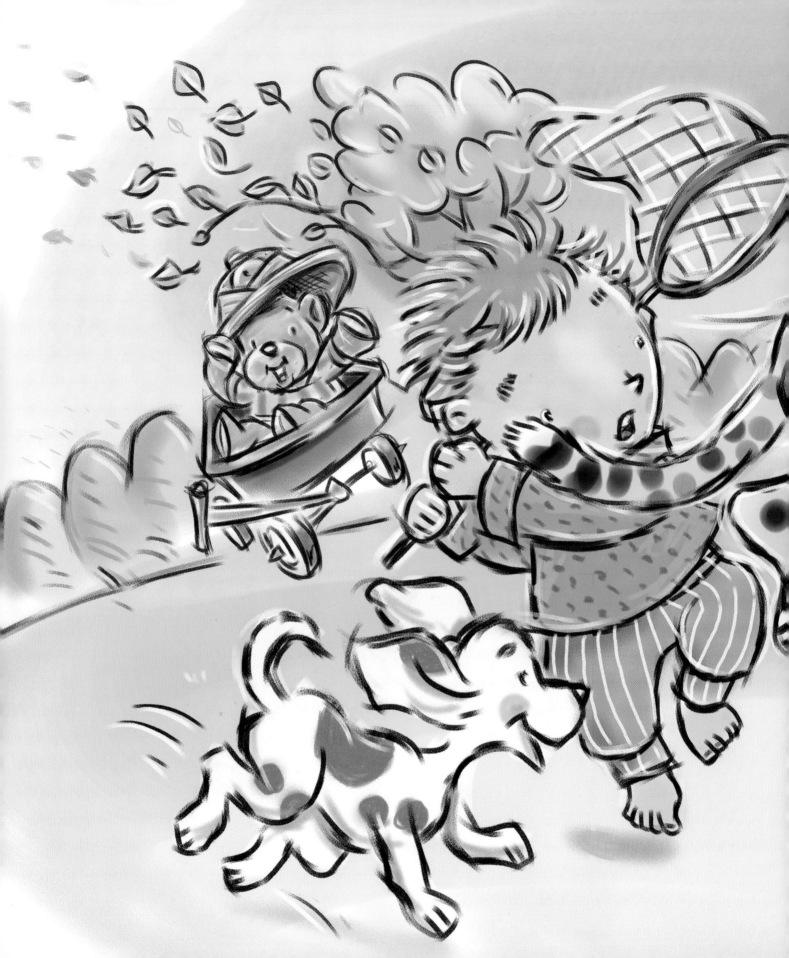

Too fast.

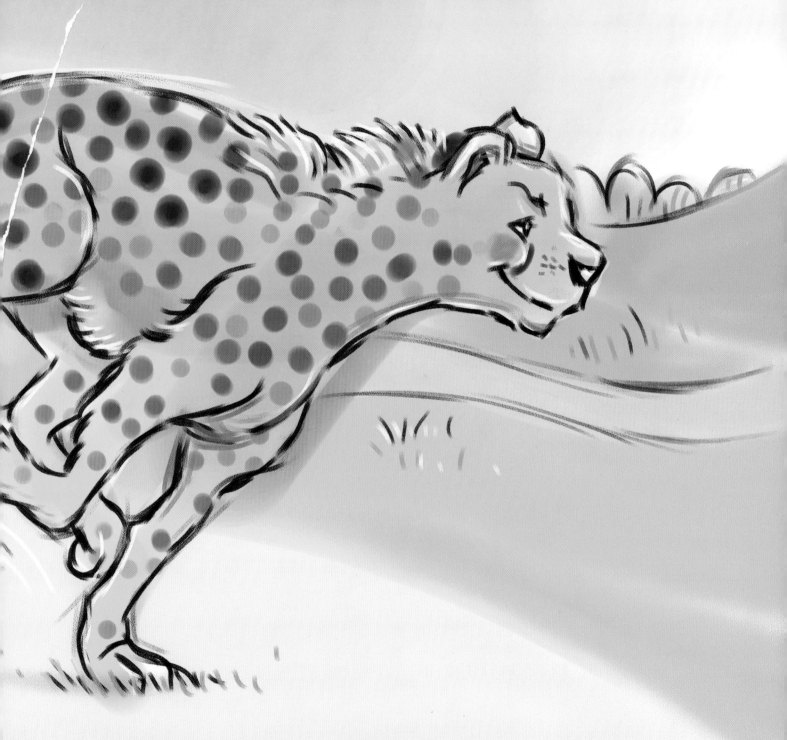

Too slow.

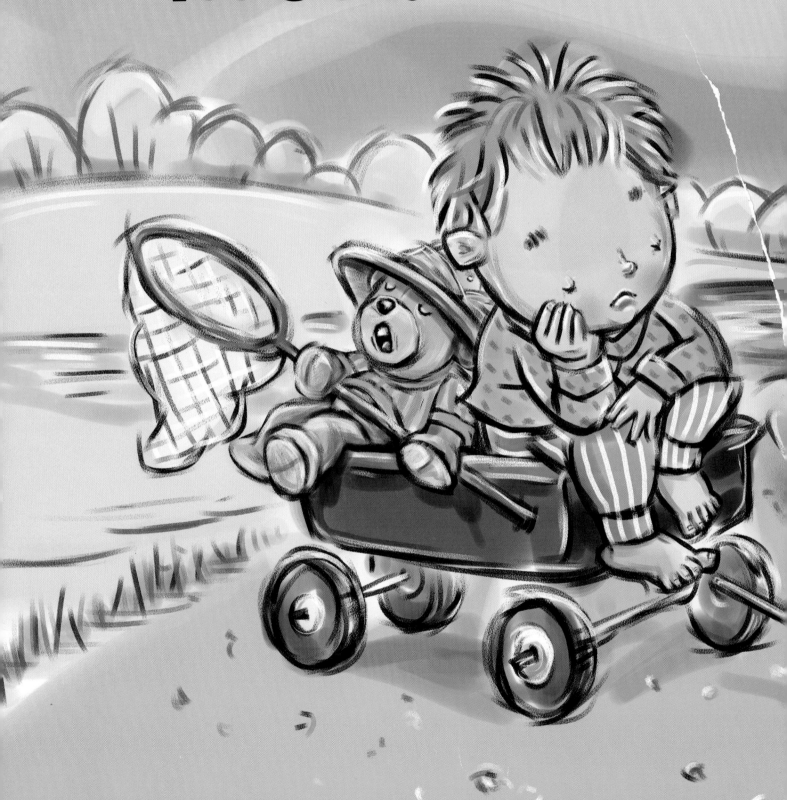

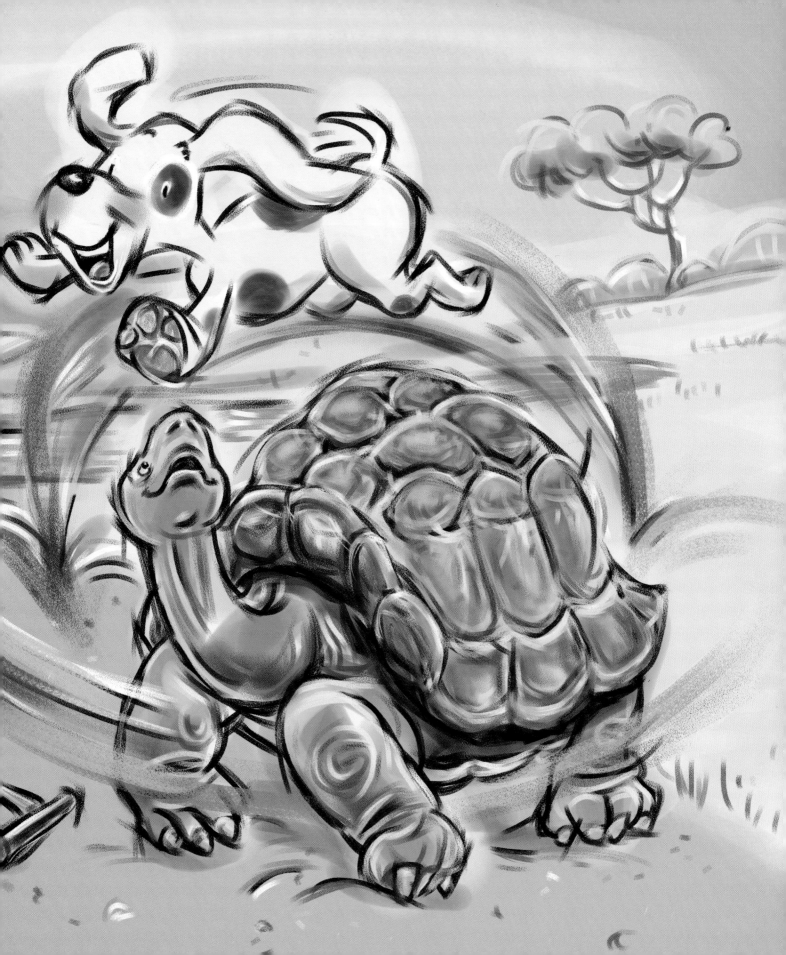

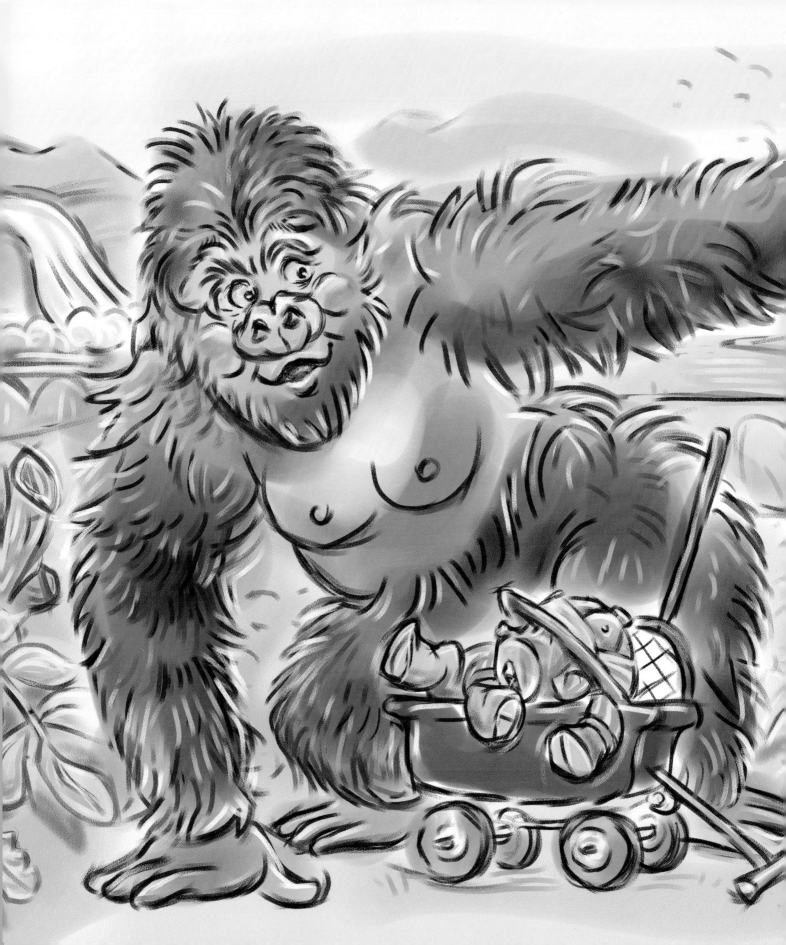

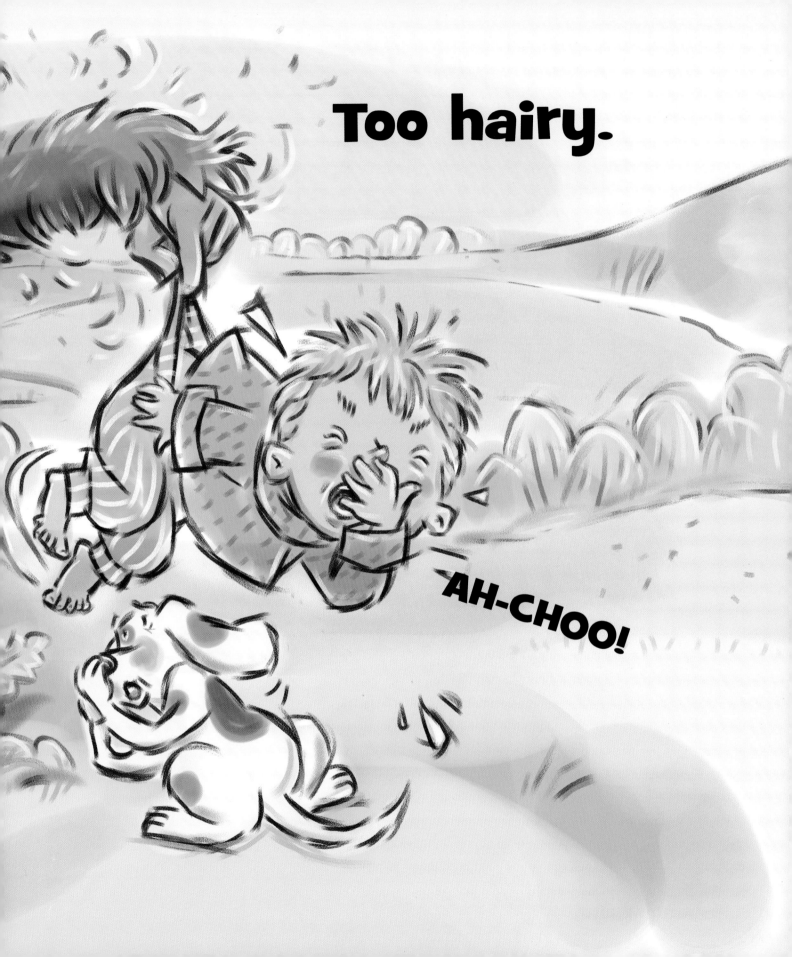

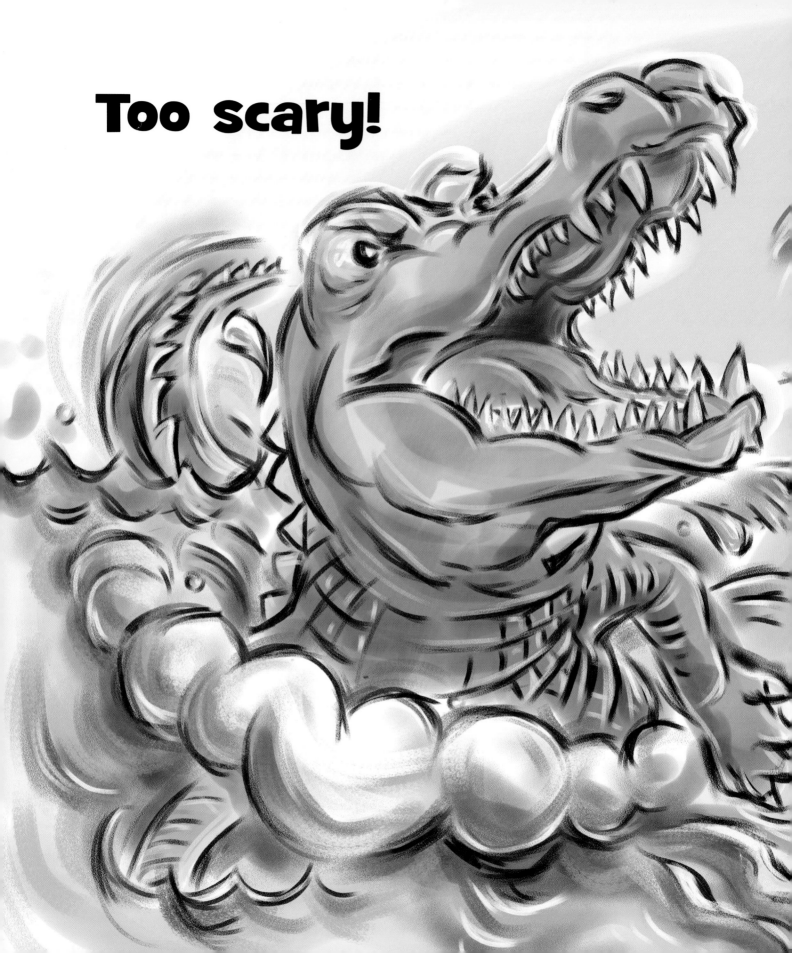

Too scary!

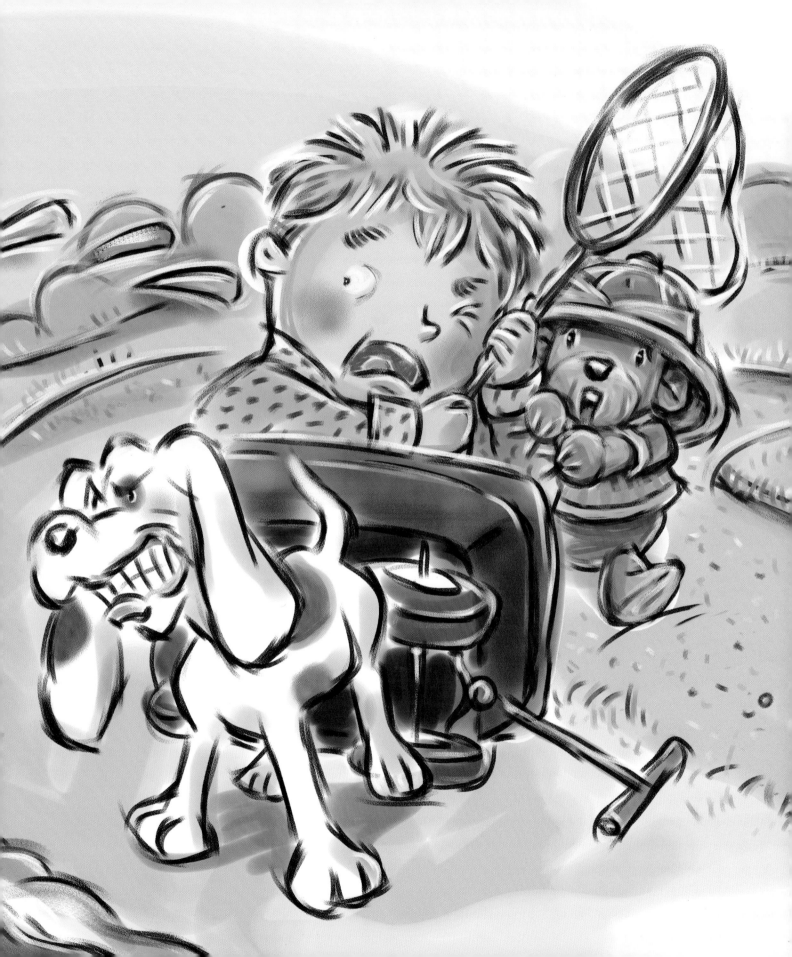

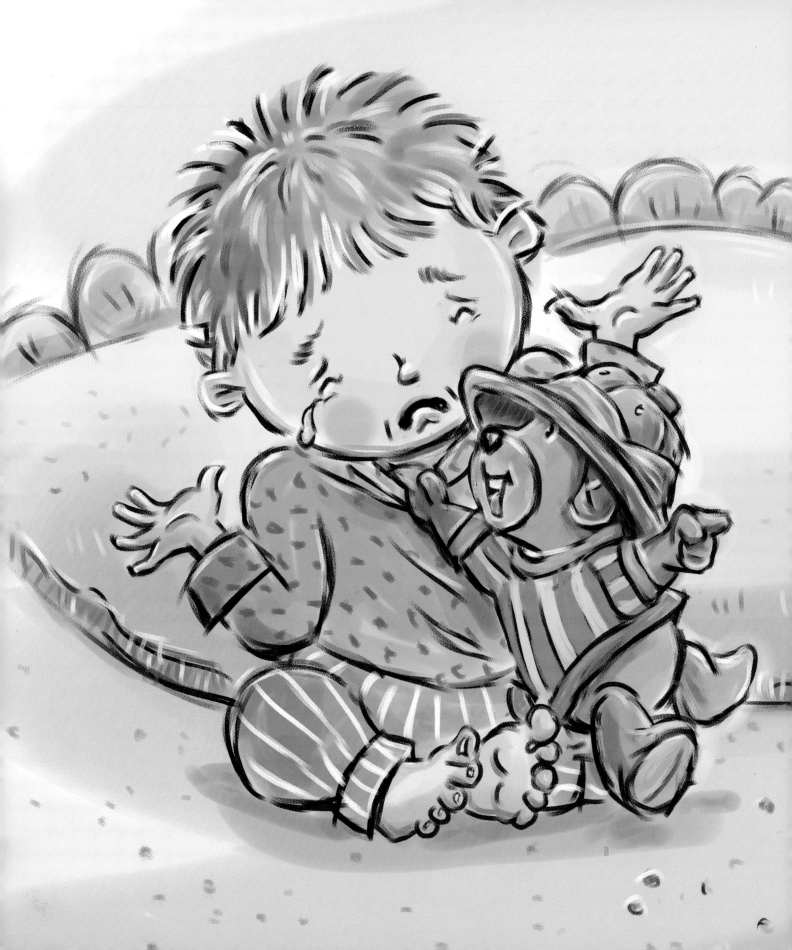

None of these will do.

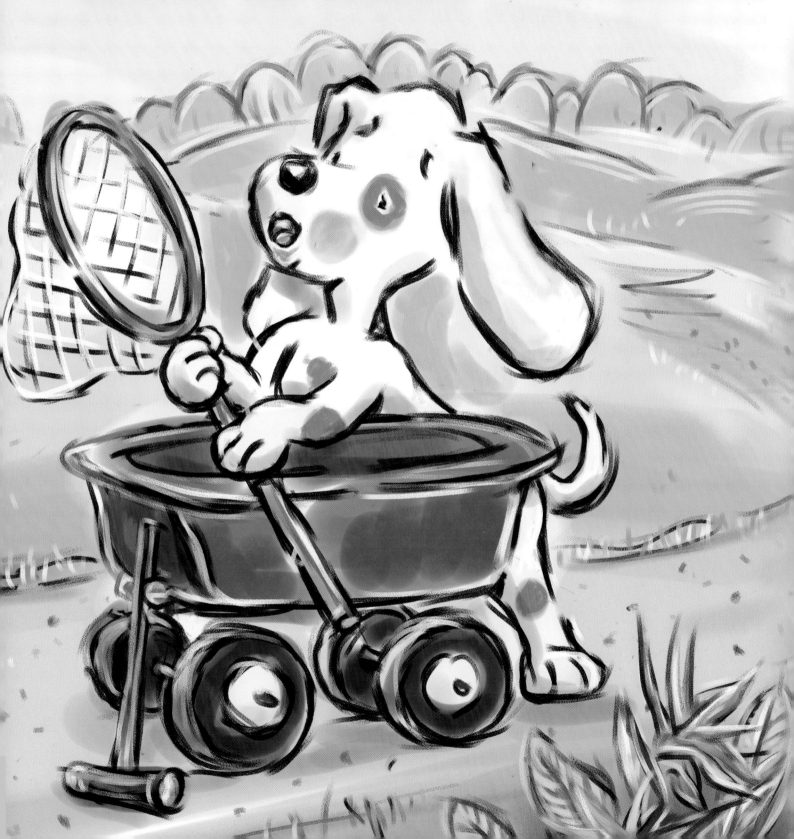

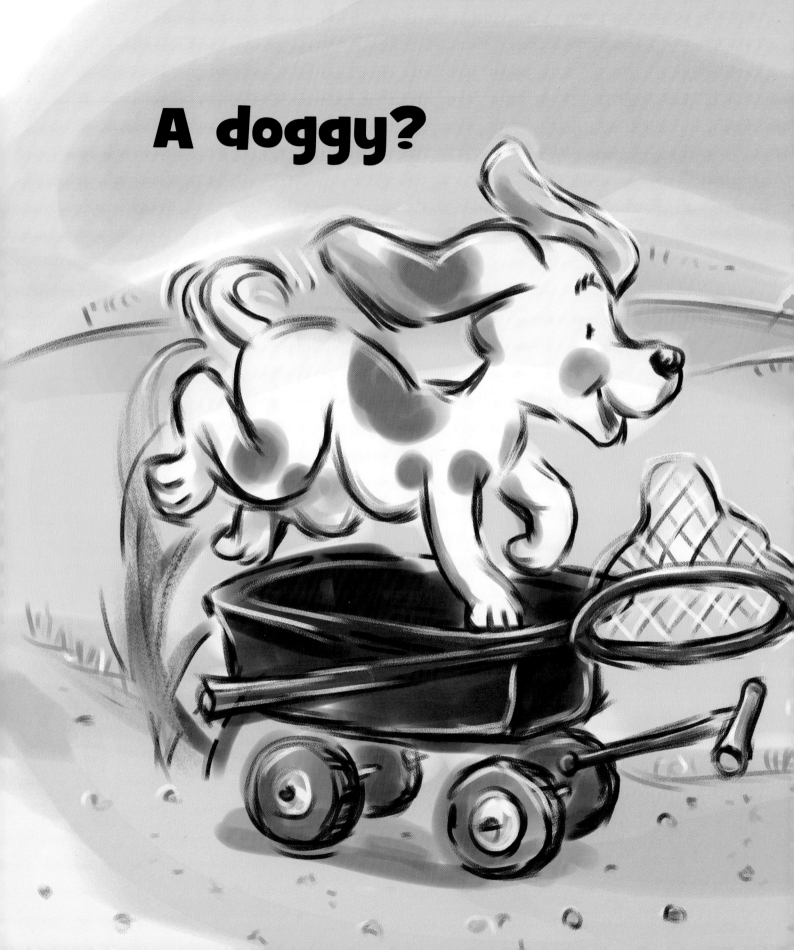

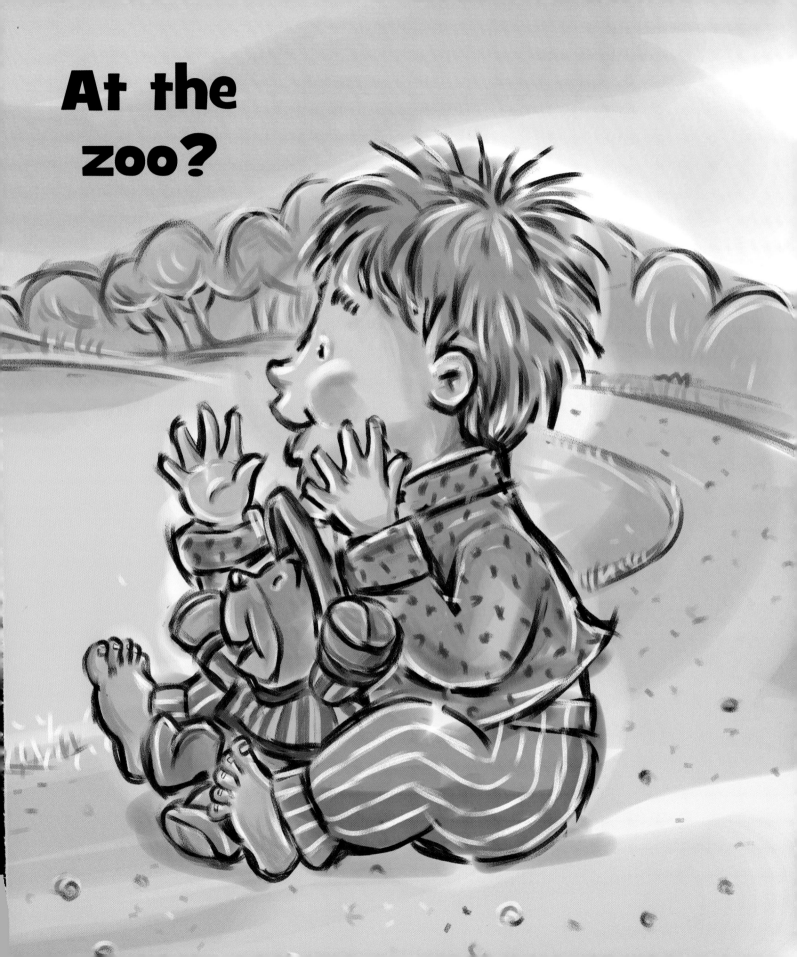

At the zoo?

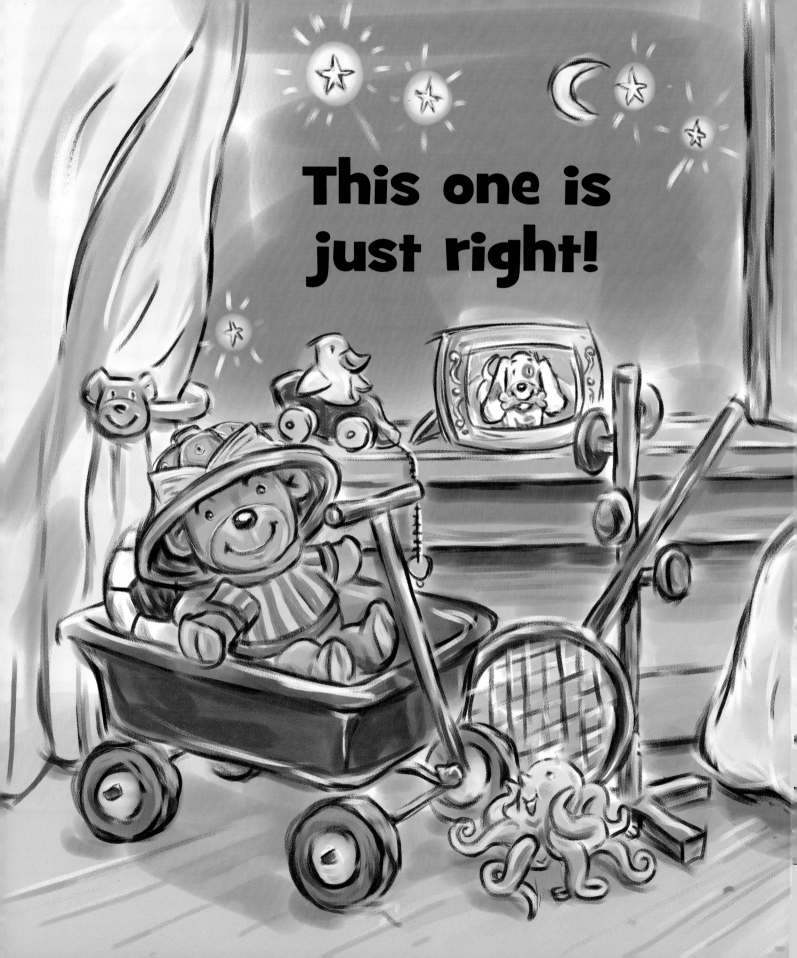

This one is
just right!

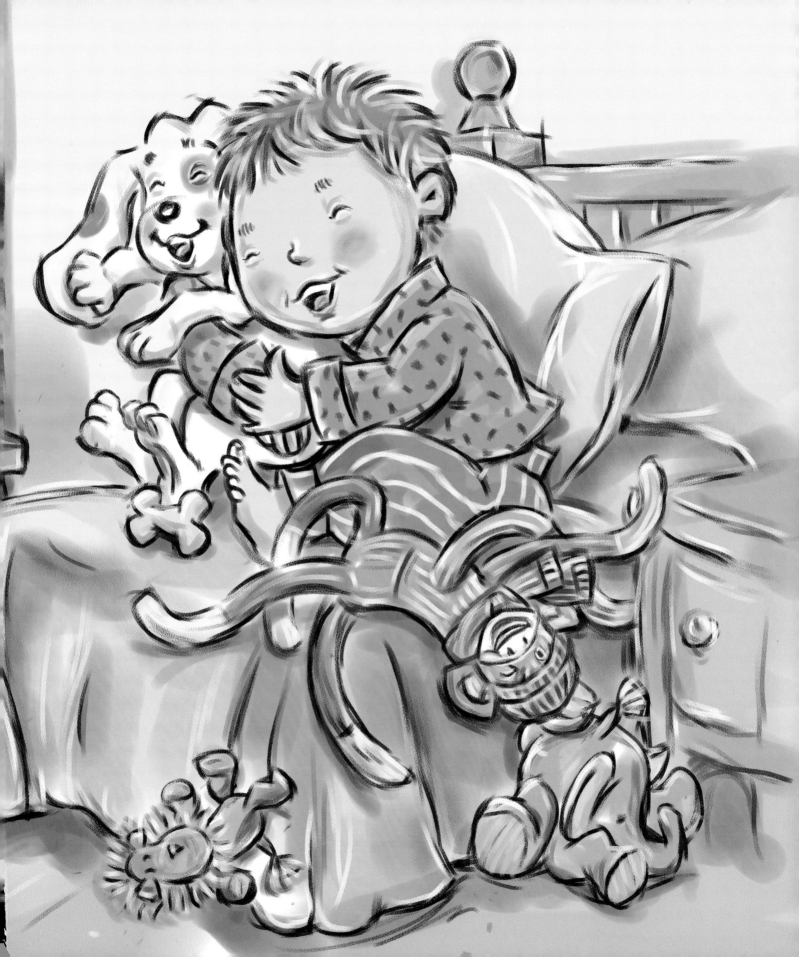

Time to go night-night.

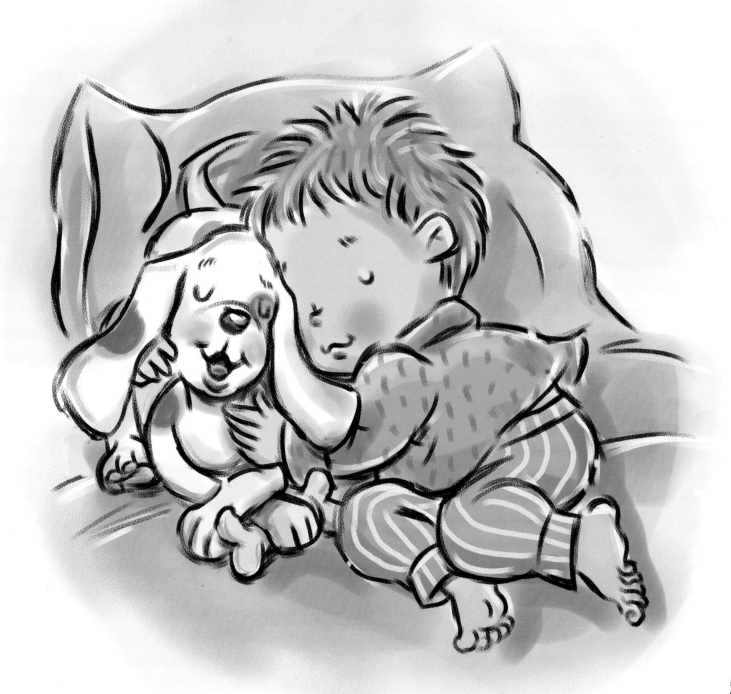